Dedicated to my nieces, Ela and Zoey.

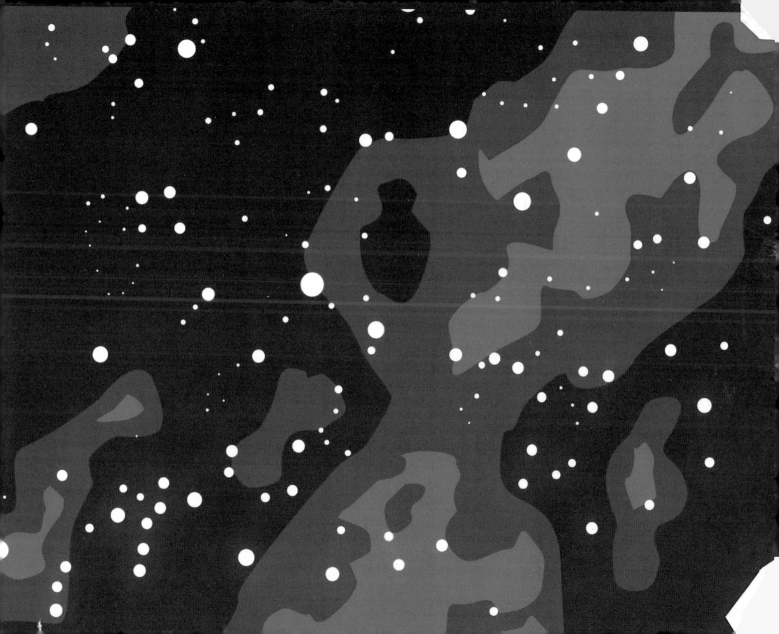

Stella and the Stars

Story and Art by Andy Wang

Twinkle, twinkle, little star,
How I wonder what you are!
Up above the world so high,
Like a diamond in the sky!

When the blazing sun is gone,
When he nothing shines upon,
Then you show your little light,
Twinkle, twinkle, all the night.

Then the traveller in the dark,
Thanks you for your tiny spark,
He could not see which way to go,
If you did not twinkle so.

In the dark blue sky you keep,
And often through my curtains peep,
For you never shut your eye,
Till the sun is in the sky.

As your bright and tiny spark,
Lights the traveller in the dark,
Though I know not what you are,
Twinkle, twinkle, little star.

- "The Star" by Jane Taylor

Twinkle, twinkle, little star
How I wonder what you are,

Up above the world so high,
Like a diamond in the sky,

"What are the stars, daddy?" asked Stella.

Father replied, "The stars are our friends. They live in the sky and watch over us."

"Way up there, they can see everything," Father said. "And each one has a story."

"Do you see that star? That's the North Star, if you ever get lost it can help you find your way back home."

Stella enjoyed city life.

...to a house in the countryside.

Stella was sad that her friends were far away back in the city.

She missed her friends and all of the fun they had together.

"It's not so bad out here," Father said.

"The night sky in the country is magical. You can see many more stars. Out here, the stars really come to life."

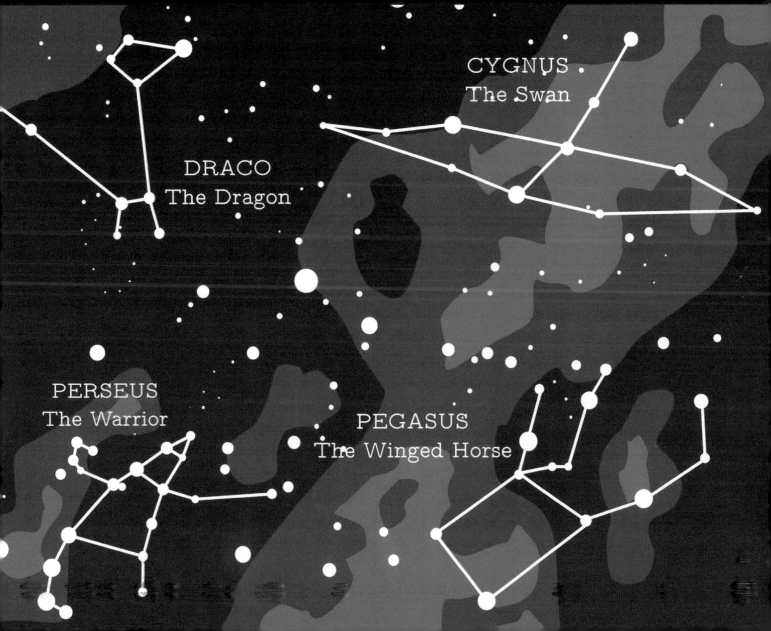

CYGNUS
The Swan

DRACO
The Dragon

PERSEUS
The Warrior

PEGASUS
The Winged Horse

"But where's the North Star?" Stella asked. "I can't find it."

Father said, "It's still there, just follow these stars of the Big Dipper, they point right to it."

"Oh, there it is!" said Stella.

"Good," said Father. "Now it's time to sleep."

When the blazing sun is gone,
When he nothing shines upon,

Then you show your little light,
Twinkle, twinkle, all the night

"Wow," said Stella. "Where am I?"

"Welcome to Cirrus!" the stars shouted.

"Hi, I'm Perseus," said the boy.
"And that's Pegasus, Draco and Cygnus."

"We all live up here with the stars.
At night, we all come out to play,"
said Draco the dragon.

Cygnus the swan asked, "Won't you join us?"

Stella played with the stars all night.

"It's almost morning," yawned Stella. "Does anyone know the way home?"

"The North Star," said Perseus. "He knows the way to everywhere."

"Are you the North Star?" Stella asked.

"Sorry, not me," a star answered.

"Are you the North Star?" Stella asked.

"Nope," said one star.

Are you the North Star?" Stella asked another star.

"Keep looking," it replied.

"How do I find him?" Stella wondered.

Then she remembered what Father said,
"Just follow the stars of the Big Dipper,
they point right to it."

"I see him!" Stella exclaimed.

"Daddy, I met the stars," Stella said.

"Now I know what they are!"

DRACO
The Dragon

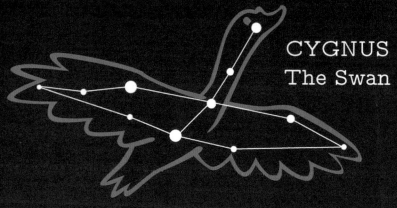

CYGNUS
The Swan

PEGASUS
The Winged Horse

PERSEUS
The Warrior

12396015R00031

Made in the USA
Lexington, KY
08 December 2011